This book is dedicated to tabby cats everywhere and the owners who love them, especially my tabbies Mork, Orange, Mac, Tiny, and Meow.

- Keri

**www.mascotbooks.com**

*The Christmas Kitten*

**For more information, please contact:**
Mascot Books
560 Herndon Parkway #120
Herndon, VA 20170
info@mascotbooks.com

Library of Congress Control Number: 2015908963

CPSIA Code: PRT0715A
ISBN-13: 978-1-63177-198-9

Printed in the United States

# The Christmas
# Kitten

written by Keri Brubaker Ems
illustrated by Terry Hinkle

T he kitten stretched, yawned, nuzzled her mother, and headed out to explore in the quiet hours of morning. She slipped past the sleeping donkey, sheep, and cattle. But this morning, it wasn't quiet.

The inn, rarely busy at this hour, was one of the kitten's favorite places. Today it felt different. Visitors were already arriving and the kitten feared she would be shooed away without any breakfast. But as she approached, Rebekah, the innkeeper's daughter, called to her, "Here, kitty, kitty! Are you hungry?"

The kitten enjoyed Rebekah's humming and stroking as she lapped the warm milk. Soon the kitten heard, "Rebekah, where are you? There's work to be done!" With a tummy full of warm milk and a squeeze from her friend, the kitten was on her way.

T he synagogue where the kitten chased mice and napped with the rabbi already had visitors, which probably meant no mice and no nap.

istracted by all the visitors, the rabbi gave the kitten
a quick scratch under her chin and behind her ears
before putting her down. The kitten wandered back
out into the early light of morning.

The market was set up and full of more people than usual. The kitten scurried out into the road, a dangerous place for a small kitten, as she darted between feet and hooves.

From out of nowhere, "WOOF, WOOF!" Running for her life, the kitten was able to escape to the safe refuge of a small tree.

With a better view of the small town, the kitten wondered, *Who are all these people and why are they here?*

At nightfall when the streets began to empty, the kitten left her watching spot and ambled back to the barn. The hungry kitten joined her momma and brothers as they lapped a saucer of warm goat's milk. Rebekah cleaned the stable, added fresh hay to the manger, and played with the kittens.

Tummy full of milk, the kitten nestled into the furry ball of her sleeping brothers. Before she drifted off to sleep, she noticed how brightly the stars shined through the stable window, especially one right over the stable, shining brightest of all.

S uddenly, the stable door banged open, awakening all the animals. The cows, lowing in fear, stamped their feet with worry. The sheep baaaaaed nervously and the kittens stirred from their snuggly sleep. Startled by the sudden intrusion, they scurried to the shadowy corners of the stable.

The innkeeper entered with a man and woman and their donkey saying, "I'm sorry the inn is full. We have no more room available. But you will be safe and warm here in the stable. The hay is clean and the animals are gentle and used to people."

The weary couple thanked the innkeeper and settled down to rest. The kitten, now wide awake, was curious about the strangers and the beautiful star that was now directly overhead. She sneaked out of the stable to investigate the bright star.

The kitten wandered to the outskirts of town to get a better look. Once in the fields, the kitten saw shepherds keeping watch over their flocks. They also noticed the star and looked up in awe as it shone directly overhead. One shepherd left his flock in the protective care of another and headed to the town following the star. He noticed the kitten in the tall grass and picked her up.

everal other townspeople, including the rabbi, were walking toward the stable. Jumping from the shepherd's arms, the kitten rushed back to the safety of her brothers and momma, hoping to share the beauty of the star with them.

As she approached the stable, she heard a baby crying. Inside, the kitten saw the man and woman kneeling beside the manger soothing a child.

The weariness on their faces changed to joy as they looked at their beautiful baby boy. Just as the kitten wondered why a baby was resting in the animals' feed trough, the man said, "Mary, he must be chilly."

Curious, the kitten jumped into the manger with the baby and curled up beside him to keep him warm. Seeing the gentle kitten, the baby stopped crying and drifted off to sleep. Pleased with her help, the woman stroked the kitten's forehead in thanks and whispered, "Ktan-to-net," which means *precious little one.*

The next morning, the kitten's brothers noticed a strange mark in the shape of an *M* on her forehead, right where Mary's fingers had brushed her fur. To this day, every tabby cat has an M-shaped mark on its forehead as a reminder of how a small tabby kitten kept Baby Jesus warm on the very first Christmas.

# About the Author

Keri has been a teacher for many years. She lives in Kirkwood, Missouri, a suburb of St. Louis, with her husband and cat. She has four wonderful children and two grandchildren with whom she spends much of her time. She enjoys sewing, gardening, reading, and baking with her granddaughter. She also loves working with children and writing stories to share with them. You can visit Keri at her website, keriems.com, or on Facebook at Keri Ems Author.

# About the Illustrator

Terry has been creating art since he was old enough to hold a crayon. He started his career as a commercial artist, illustrator, and designer but quickly moved to the creative business of advertising and promotion as an art director/creative director. Now Terry enjoys focusing his talents on children's books and his painting.

Terry lives in Kirkwood, Missouri with his wife, two daughters, cat, and dog. He and Keri have been friends for many years and plan to do more books together. You can visit Terry on Facebook at HinkleArt.